SACRED PLACES

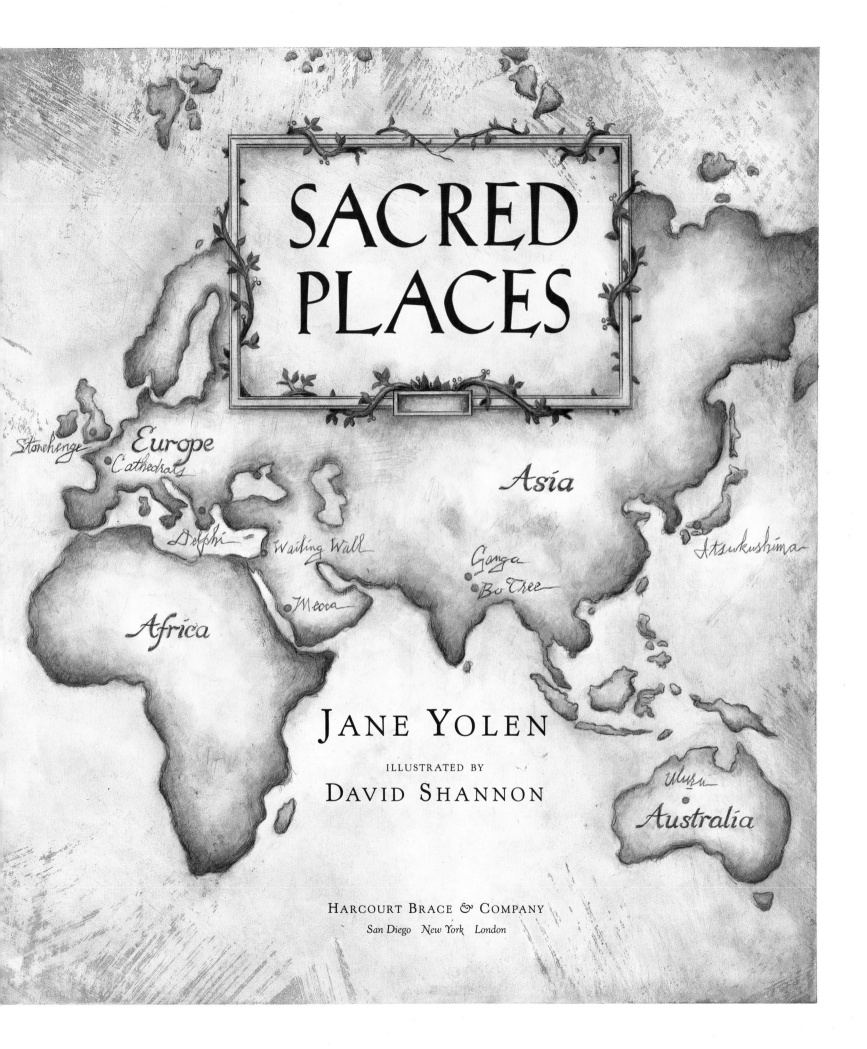

SACRED PLACES

Stonehenge
Europe
Cathedrals
Delphi
Waiting Wall
Africa
Asia
Mecca
Ganga
Bo Tree
Itsukushima
Uluru
Australia

JANE YOLEN

ILLUSTRATED BY
DAVID SHANNON

HARCOURT BRACE & COMPANY
San Diego New York London

Library of Congress Cataloging-in-Publication Data
Yolen, Jane.
Sacred places/Jane Yolen; illustrated by David Shannon.—1st ed.
p.   cm.
Summary: A collection of poems about different places around the
world that are considered sacred by various cultures, including
Mecca, the Ganges River, and Christian cathedrals.
ISBN 0-15-269953-8
1. Sacred space—Juvenile poetry. 2. Children's poetry, American.
3. Religious poetry, American. [1. Sacred space—Poetry.
2. American poetry.]   I. Shannon, David, 1959–   ill.   II. Title.
PS3575.O43S3   1996
811'.54—dc20   92-30323

Printed in Singapore
First edition
A B C D E

For Tim Peck, idea man;
and for David, who has gone with me
to many of these sacred places

—J. Y.

To my wife, Heidi;
and to Lois, who makes Every Picture
a sacred place

—D. S.

Contents

Hush,
this is a holy place,
a sacred place,
where the visions dwell,
where the dreaming
of a race began.
Someone's God
has stepped here,
slept here,
knelt here,
dwelt here,
spoken here of life, of death,
of holy things.
When you come,
come softly,
walk softly,
talk softly,
be mindful of the dreams.
This place is a sacred place.
Hush.

DELPHI

Two eagles, sharp of beak and eye,
wings wide as the sun,
found the earth's center,
the earth's own navel,
Omphalos.
And there Apollo,
divine Apollo,
snake-killer, sun-rider,
fosterer of flocks Apollo,
set his speaker of truths,
set his prophet and seer,
set his oracle, Pythia.

"Answer what shall be asked," he told her.
"Speak what must be spoken," he told her.

And from the perfumed cave,
from the earth's dark center,
from the navel of the world
she spoke truth.

But what is truth?
Is it the words spoken?
Is it the words heard?
Or does truth lie
somewhere between
the mouth and ear,
here
in the earth's center,
here
in the earth's navel,
here
in the oracle's cave.

COPÁN

Let the priests speak of time;
let them regulate the days;
let them tell us when to build
and when to reap,
when to sue for peace
and when to make war.
Let them count
on the fingers of four hands
and mark those counts
upon the stairs.

Stone upon stone,
bring us to Father Sun.
Stone upon stone,
bring us to Mother Moon.

Let the kings speak in blood;
let them put piercers in their tongues;
let them lead the jaguar hunt,
and choose the sacrifice,
and wed their sisters,
and wear the quetzal tail.
Let them file
their teeth to points
and ornament them with
hematite and jade.

Stone upon stone,
bring us to Father Sun.
Stone upon stone,
bring us to Mother Moon.

Let the people speak of the gods;
let them pray for rain to Chac;
let them cry for corn and good soil,
and play with the rubber ball,
and weave cotton blankets,
and wear earrings of obsidian and wood.
Let them live
in single huts in the forest
where the hearth smoke
escapes through the palm-thatched roof.

Stone upon stone,
bring us to Father Sun.
Stone upon stone,
bring us to Mother Moon.

WAILING WALL

On the eve of the ninth day
of the month of Av
we come to Jerusalem,
we come to the Wall.
At my left hand a black-coated Hasid nodding.
At my right an armed soldier weeping.
Hear, O Israel.
Here, O Israel,
in the dead of night,
a dove as white as hope,
a dove as white as truth
sighs its sorrow into the darkling air.
The water on the Wall's top
is not dew, is not rain.
The Wall weeps for us,
for the destruction of the Temple,
for the destruction of the People.
I place a prayer into a cleft
for those who are left
here, O Israel.
Hear, O Israel,
the sounds of lamentations
and the rending of fine cloth.

Easter Island

Eyes of stone stare
unblinking in the sun's fierce glare.
Heads of stone ride burial walls
like terns atop
the rise and fall of an ocean wave.
Whose hands did carve,
did care, did save,
did pry, did live, did die
to pull these gods
from the crater's well?
Only mouths of stone can tell.

STONEHENGE

The roving people counted moons,
The settled used the sun;
But here eternity's clock is timed
By summer's shadow through the stones.

Who worshipped here within the round?
Who danced the fairy ring?
Whose priestly voices called the tunes?
Whose bodies from the stones were hung?

Earthworks these are, and Earth's remain,
The barrows bound and point
To worlds in worlds we scarcely know
That rain and mist and sun anoint.

GANGA

We come more numerous than the gulls
to ride the waves;
we come more numerous than the sacred cows
to drink the water;
we come more numerous than the black beetles
to walk the sands,
but not more precious.
For all life is one life,
and all life ends
here at the river,
and begins.
Sing Rama,
sing Mother Parvati,
dance for us Lord Shiva,
Krishna play upon your flute.
The waters make us pure.

ULURU

Here in the red center
rises up the great red rock,
Uluru.
It is a place of men;
it is a place of women;
it is a place of ancestors
who left their marks
on every scar and escarpment,
every water hole and wind hole,
every rock face and feature,
every weather and creature.
It is a rock of stories
and histories,
a rock that holds memories.
The rock remembers the Dreamtime
when the hare-wallaby people
were savaged by the black dog Kurpany
and the kingfisher cried warning, but too late.
It remembers the Dreamtime
when the python woman of power Kuniya
killed her upstart nephew
with a mighty blow,
and her anger so poisoned the plants,
spearwood still bears it to this day.

The rock records the tales
that we may read and remember,
here in the red center
where the peregrine falcon
still hunts on the hot winds,
and the blue-tongue lizard
looks out from the rock folds,
and the hare-wallaby hurries by,
the day before today,
and today,
and again the day after.

CATHEDRALS

Orléans,
St. Denis,
Notre-Dame,
And damp St. Mark's.

This is the crypt,
This the nave,
This the apse,
These the graves.

Chartres and Ely,
Martin of Tours,
The stones recount
The building years.

Through the rose,
Through the rose,
Through the rose
The light of God shows.

Old St. Peter's,
Apollinare,
Fulda and Nevers,
The hours near.

One for father,
One for son,
One for spirit,
All are one.

This is the crypt,
This the nave,
This the apse,
These the graves.

The mass is ended.
Let us go in peace.

Bo Tree

There are many roads
through the forest.
There are many ways
through the trees.
The middle path
leads to the Bo,
and under its branches
the enlightened rest.

There was a prince of warriors
gave up his kingdom.
There was a hermit in the forest
lost among trees.
They were two but they were one;
they found the path
by sitting still.

Can not moonlight
gleam on a thousand waters?
Can not sun cast shadows
of a thousand thousand trees?

Are these riddles?
They have no answers
except you find them
as the Buddha did,
on a couch of grass,
facing east, untempted,
under the spreading branches
of the pipal,
under the long-stemmed leaves
of the Enlightenment Tree.

MECCA

Stories within stories,
the pilgrims hear
of the holy city
where the prophet was born,
where he spoke the prophecies,
where he gave the law.
Stories upon stories,
the pilgrims hear
of Hagar and Ismael
who nearly died,
and of the house like God's own
that Ibrahim built.
Stories within stories,
the pilgrims hear
of the God-sent stone
black as any night,
black as the prophet's own hair.
Stories within stories,
the pilgrims hear
and come through Jidda,
across dry *wadis*,
flocking to that city,
to that house,
to that stone,
adding their own stories
to the litany of the years.

FOUR CORNERS

North is here,
the wind's teeth and belly.
South is here,
teasing corn and maidens.
East is here,
the sound of the mule deer.
West is here,
thundering like a thousand thousand buffalo.
These are the four ways
at the four corners
we can see with the eye.
But life is never so simple.
There is still up,
there is still down,
there are the many roads between
earth lodge and white man's border,
many songs between
the hoe and field,
many cries between
the arrow and its prey.

ITSUKUSHIMA

High Tide

The little waves lap the pillars,
see-swash, see-swash, see-swash.
It is the voice of Shiho-tsuchi,
it is the song of Oho-wata-tsu-mi,
lords of the ocean realm.
O lords, we pray to be saved from shipwreck,
we pray to be safe from giant waves.
Send your messengers,
the crocodile and shark.
We will greet them with great pleasure.
We will show them our great fear.

Low Tide

The mud path through the pillars
makes a sucking sound
beneath our thonged sandals.
It is the disgust of Shiho-tsuchi, . . .
it is the anger of Oho-wata-tsu-mi,
lords of the ocean realm.
Is it here they keep the jewels
that regulate the tides,
here beneath the mud, under the gateway,
with the skies as blue
as springs feeding into the widening sea?

Hush,

this is a holy place,

a sacred place,

where the visions dwell,

where the dreaming

of a race began.

Someone's God

has stepped here,

slept here,

knelt here,

dwelt here,

spoken here of life, of death,

of holy things.

Since you have been here,

truth has been shaped,

truth has been shifted,

truth has been shown

in its many forms.

All truths.

One truth.

So walk softly,

talk softly,

be mindful of the dreams.

This place is a sacred place.

Hush.

More about the Sacred Places

DELPHI: The oracle at Delphi operated for more than one thousand years, and during the sixth and seventh centuries B.C., people came from all over the world to visit the sacred shrine and ask questions of importance. The answers they got from the Pythia, a woman in a trance, were mysterious, a little like riddles. Legend states that it was the god Apollo himself who set up the first oracle at the shrine. Another myth tells how two eagles, loosed by Zeus, located the navel of the world, or *Omphalos,* at Delphi.

COPÁN: The Mayan peoples of Central and South America built several massive ceremonial centers, including this one in Honduras. These were centers of worship and government, and included pyramids and enormous ball courts. Many of the buildings and the great stone steps leading up to them were covered with hieroglyphs, picture writing carved into the stone. The staircase illustrated here contains more than twelve hundred hieroglyphs, which record the exploits of fifteen kings. The Mayan priests kept complex calendars and counted by twenties, not by tens as we do. The royal families practiced ritual bloodletting, both on themselves and, occasionally, by sacrificing human captives or slaves.

WAILING WALL: In the Old City of Jerusalem is one of the Jewish people's most sacred sites. Called in Hebrew *ha-Kotel ha-Ma'aravi,* or Western Wall, it has been known familiarly as the Wailing Wall for many years. Visible today is a remnant of the wall that surrounded the Temple Mount in the last century B.C. Of the original twenty-four layers of rock, only seven remain above ground. For generations Jews have made pilgrimages here, especially on Tishah b'Av, the eve of the ninth day of the month of Av, the fast day commemorating the destruction of the First and Second Temples. The prayer that is the watchword of the Jewish faith is the *Shema:* "Hear O Israel, the Lord Our God, the Lord is One."

EASTER ISLAND: On Easter Sunday 1722, Dutch admiral Jacob Roggeveen sailed his ship to a volcanic island known by the natives as Rapa Nui. All over the island were enormous stone statues, massive heads, many atop stone platforms called *ahus.* The statues number about a thousand and are as high as thirty-two feet. The stone had all been quarried from a volcano on the northeast end of the island, and it remains a mystery how such a primitive and metal-poor people could have moved the great stone statues, carved from single stones, so far. Or why.

STONEHENGE: A circle of standing stones on Salisbury Plain in England, Stonehenge was probably built for worship or as a celestial calendar. Scholars have debated its use for years. The word *henge* in Saxon means "hanging," and some investigators believe the pagan Saxons hung human sacrifices on the stones; others believe the word simply refers to the hanging or lintel stones across the top. Manmade barrows or mounds are found in the vicinity, and while some are clearly burial sites, not all are. The largest, Silbury Hill, remains mysterious.

GANGA: The Ganges, the great river of Northern India, receives hundreds of thousands of Hindu pilgrims each year. Although there are *tirthas* (holy rivers) throughout India, those sites on the Ganges are considered most sacred. Rama, Parvati, Shiva, and Krishna are among the many gods worshipped in India: Rama as the ideal ruler and an incarnation of the great god Vishnu; Parvati, the Mother Goddess and bestower of blessings; Shiva, Lord of the Dance, who directs the movement of all material things; Krishna who, with his divine flute, calls to the human soul.

ULURU: This great rock, five miles around, dominates the red earth landscape of Central Australia. The area's Aboriginal people still perform religious ceremonies on and around the rock as they have for more than ten thousand years. Like other natural features in Australia, Uluru is a map of the myths of the Aboriginal Dreamtime, the Creation, when ancestral beings crossed the world leaving marks in the form of streams, hills, rocks, and caves. In the late 1800s, white settlers took the land and renamed Uluru "Ayers Rock." In 1985 title was given back to the Aboriginal owners, who now run the area as a national park.

CATHEDRALS: The names of the hundreds of cathedrals built around the world to the glory of Christ ring like a poem. Cathedral building really began with the great stone basilicas—like old St. Peter's in Rome—constructed after the church achieved legal status in A.D. 313. Some of the most beautiful features of many cathedrals are the stained-glass windows. Some tell stories from the Bible and some—like the magnificent thirteenth-century rose window at Chartres—are more abstract.

BO TREE: The bo or bodhi tree, a pipal or sacred fig tree, is located in Bōdh Gayā, Bīhar, India, and has been sacred to Buddhists for nearly 2,400 years. Hundreds of thousands of pilgrims have visited it, making offerings and pouring libations at its roots. The faithful believe this is a descendant of the actual tree that Gautama Buddha sat under in the sixth century B.C. when he attained enlightenment and understood the ways of the world— which became the teachings of Buddhism.

MECCA: The place of the great *hajj,* or pilgrimage, was set by the prophet Muhammad. Mecca was his birthplace, and today only the Muslim faithful can enter the city. Before entering Mecca, pilgrims prepare by bathing, clipping the hair and nails, and changing into special, seamless clothes that consist of one (for women) or two (for men) sheets of white cloth. The pilgrims go seven times around the Ka'ba, the cubelike sacred shrine of Islam that is covered by a great embroidered cloth. The Ka'ba, the geographic center of Islam, is in the courtyard of the Great Mosque, and in the Ka'ba's eastern corner is embedded the Black Stone, which the pilgrims must kiss.

FOUR CORNERS: Where New Mexico, Colorado, Arizona, and Utah meet is the place often referred to as Four Corners. According to many Native American groups, it is the place where the directions originated and go outward; different colors are associated with different directions. Today the Native people who live in the area are mostly Navajo, Ute, Jicarilla, Apache, and Pueblo. While this poem does not refer to specific tribal customs, it is patterned after some of the Navajo and Hopi songs.

ITSUKUSHIMA: The gateway (or *torii*) of the Shinto shrine at Itsukushima is surrounded by water at high tide and is in the middle of a mudflat at low tide. This Japanese shrine is dedicated to the gods of the sea, most prominent of whom are Oho-wata-tsu-mi, whose messenger is the shark, and Shiho-tsuchi, whose messenger is the crocodile. The gods also control the jewels that regulate the tides.

The illustrations in this book were done in
acrylic paint on illustration board.
The display type was set in Celestia Antigua.
The text type was set in Kennerly by
Thompson Type, San Diego, California.
Color separations by Bright Arts, Ltd., Singapore
Printed and bound by Tien Wah Press, Singapore
This book was printed with soya-based inks on Leykam recycled paper,
which contains more than 20 percent postconsumer waste and has
a total recycled content of at least 50 percent.
Production supervision by Warren Wallerstein
and Ginger Boyer
Designed by Lisa Peters